The ... of Robin's Toys

Ken and Angie Lake

Roger the Reindeer

Published by Sweet Cherry Publishing Limited
53 St. Stephens Road,
Leicester, LE2 1GH
United Kingdom

First Published in the UK in 2013

ISBN: 978-1-78226-030-1
Text: © Ken and Angie Lake 2013
Illustrations: (c) Vishnu Madhav,
Creative Books

Printed and Bound By Nutech Print Services, India

Every Toy Has a Story to Tell

Have you ever seen an old toy, perhaps in a cupboard, or in the attic or loft? Have you ever seen how sad they look at car boot sales, unwanted and unloved? Well, look at them closely, because every toy has a story to tell, and the older, the more decrepit, the more scruffy, the more tatty the toy is, the more interesting its story could be. Here are just a few of those toys and their stories.

16th December, 09.25

It was Sunday morning, and Robin stared out of the window at a heavy, dark sky. A cold wind blew down the street and people hurried along, wrapped in their warm winter clothes.

Then something really wonderful happened. There were just a few flakes at first, floating along with the wind. Then there were more and more. Soon the street had a

dusting of pure white snow.
It looked like a winter
wonderland. Wow, great!

Robin knew that it would
soon be Christmas and he was
thinking about what present he
could get for Grandad.

He had already made him a Christmas card at school, but he wanted to give him a special present because Grandad had been very kind. Every Sunday he took Robin to the car boot sale and gave him 50 pence to spend on a toy. Then Grandad worked his magic and the toy would tell them a story.

Robin looked back over his week at school; it had been a strange week. There was a new girl in class called Alicia. She was Italian, and her family had

moved to England last year
when her dad got a new job.

Alicia just couldn't get used to life in England at all; she had already moved schools twice in the same year!

She didn't speak to anyone or pay any attention to the teacher, and she didn't hand in any homework. When Miss Green asked her to read aloud, she just turned her head and looked out of the window.

Miss Green had spoken to her parents, but they said that Alicia was still sad about having to leave her friends in Italy. Alicia said that as soon as she was old enough she would go back there, so she refused to learn English.

As Robin waited, he did his favourite thing - drawing. He drew so often that he was becoming quite good at it. Today he was drawing the street, with Grandad's little red car driving along it.

Now I shall draw a Christmas tree somewhere in the picture, he thought. When he looked up, he saw that it had stopped snowing, and then suddenly, Grandad's little red car appeared in the street.

Beep, beep! Beep, beep!

"Come on, Robin, it's time to go to the car boot sale."

"Hello, Grandad. I didn't think that you would come in the snow."

"Oh, Robin, I wouldn't miss taking you to the car boot sale for all the tea in China."

Robin had never thought about the amount of tea in China, but he assumed that there must be a lot.

When they arrived, some
of the people had gone home,
but there were still lots of
stalls.

"Alright, Robin, let's go and see my old friend Ian Fraser. His stall is always here."

Mr Fraser was in his usual place with his bargain foods stall, Fraser's Foods. He owned a little shop next to the Post Office and used the car boot sale stall to sell off food which he couldn't sell in the shop, like dented tins of baked beans.

Sometimes, Robin would look in the damaged case and find broken biscuits or half-melted chocolate bars. Robin loved broken biscuits, because he could just open the packet and pour the contents into his mouth.

Grandad had shown him this trick, but ever since Grandma caught them guzzling down a packet of broken chocolate chip cookies, they had been banned from buying anything from Mr Fraser.

She said that it was disgusting and dangerous, but they suspected she just didn't like all the crumbs they left on the carpet.

"Good morning, Ian,"
Grandad said as he walked up
to the stall and looked into the
damaged case.

"Good morning, Harry,
good morning, Robin," he
answered. "I have lots of
damaged biscuits this week;
that new boy at my shop
managed to break a whole case

of them. He said that he fell over the cat, but I have my doubts."

"Oh, that's terrible, Ian. Were there any injuries?"

"Yes, there certainly were. The whole case of biscuits was broken."

"And was the cat alright?"

"Harry, we don't have a cat.
So how about some broken
biscuits?"

"Sorry, Ian, but Mabel has
banned us from buying them."

"Well, if she changes her mind, let me know. These won't go off until March."

"What else have you got?"

"We have some leaky shampoo bottles, some damaged cleaning products ... Actually, I have quite a lot of stuff this week; the new boy is very clumsy. On his first day he crashed his bicycle into the shop window, fell off and broke his glasses.

"On his second day, he
was riding his bicycle without
his glasses on and he crashed

into the delivery man."

"I don't know if I really need any leaky bottles of shampoo..."

"Well, you know where to find me if you change your mind!"

"Alright, Ian. Cheerio!"

Robin and Grandad walked off to look for a toy.

"How do you know Mr Fraser-Foods, Grandad?"

"Well, Robin, we were in a rock band together."

"Really, Grandad? I didn't know you were in a rock band. What were you called?"

"We went under several names, but we were mostly known as Hell's Grandads."

"Wow! That's really cool."

"Okay, Robin, who shall we try next?"

"I know, let's have a look at Ben's Odds and Ends."

As Christmas was coming, Ben had lots of Christmas things on his stall, like fancy wrapping paper, and bits of tinsel and baubles to decorate the Christmas tree. But Robin couldn't see many toys, so he asked the owner of the stall.

"Err, excuse me, but do you have any toys this week?"

"No, not many, but I do have this one. He is sort of appropriate for this time of year."

He reached behind the stall and picked up one of the cutest reindeers that Robin had ever seen.

"This, young man, is Roger the Reindeer. I bet you thought his name was going to be Rudolf, didn't you?"

"Not exactly, Mr Odds and Ends; he doesn't have a red nose."

"Ah yes, very funny, young man."

"I shall ask my grandad to have a close look at him."

Grandad picked up Roger the Reindeer and used his magic powers to see if he had an interesting story to tell.

"What do you think about him, Grandad?"

"Yes, Robin, I think he has lots to tell us. Ask the man how much he costs."

"How much does Roger cost?"

"Oh, as it's nearly Christmas, you can have him for only 50 pence."

"Thank you very much."

"Shall I put Roger the Reindeer in a bag for you?"

After they had bought the reindeer, Grandad had to buy a present for Grandma. You see, every week he would bring her back a special surprise from the car boot sale, whether she wanted it or not (usually she didn't).

They had a look around, but didn't see anything interesting. Then Grandad had an idea.

"I know just the thing!" he said. "Let's go back to Ian Fraser's stall."

"Ian," said Grandad, "you don't happen to have any broom heads, do you?"

"Well, Harry, it just so happens that I do! They were full brooms at the beginning of the week, but the new boy ran over them with his bicycle when he went out to buy some new glasses. Shall I put one in a bag for you?"

Robin and Grandad had bought everything they wanted and could now go back to Grandad's house for a cup of tea. It was freezing outside, so it was lovely to open the front door and be greeted by the smell of fresh baking.

"Hello, boys," Grandma said from the kitchen.

"Hello there, Grandma. Something smells nice!"

"I've made you some mince pies to have with your tea."

"Oh great! I love mince pies," answered Robin.

"And we have something
for you, dear," said Grandad,
handing over the bag.

Grandma looked inside the
bag.

"Oh, Harry, I didn't expect
this! My old broom has lasted

so well. I've had it since we were married, and it's only had 16 new heads and 9 new handles!"

Then Grandma went to call one of her friends, while Robin and Grandad sat in the kitchen to have their tea. Robin put Roger the Reindeer on the kitchen table and Grandad said his magic spell.

"Little toy, hear this rhyme,
Let it take you back in time,
Tales of sadness or of glory,
Little toy, reveal your story."

Roger blinked his eyes, shook his antlers and made a snorting noise.

"Hello, who are you?"

"Well, my name is Robin and this is my grandad."

"Oh, I am very pleased to meet you. My name is Roger."

"Yes, we know. Would you like to tell us something interesting about yourself?"

"Oh yes, Robin, I certainly would. But first, do you know what the Daddy reindeer said to the Mummy reindeer?"

"Err, no, Roger, what did the Daddy reindeer say to the Mummy reindeer?"

He gazed upwards and said, *"I think it's going to ... rain dear!"*

Then Roger did his little reindeer laugh.

"Ha! Ha! Ha! Now that I have told that old joke, let me tell you a little bit about reindeers in general.

"We all come from very cold areas like the Arctic and sub-Arctic, where we live in very large herds. In North America, we are sometimes called Caribou. We all grow antlers; even my sisters have them, but of course they are not as good or as big as mine."

Roger lifted his head and strutted around the table, showing off his antlers.

"But of course we are most famous for pulling Santa's sleigh at Christmas. That's a really difficult job, and only very special reindeers are chosen.

"Anyway, let me tell you something about myself.
I grew up in Lapland. Just in case you don't know, that's an area which stretches across the north of Norway, Sweden, Finland and even parts of Russia.

"I was born there and had lived there all my life, and I didn't know anywhere else. I spent all of my days mooching around and eating moss.

"To be honest with you, I was a bit lazy at reindeer school, and please don't tell anyone else this, but I found reading quite difficult so I didn't bother to learn properly. When I was faced with reading something, I made excuses, like I had forgotten my glasses. This made the other reindeers laugh because reindeers don't actually wear glasses.

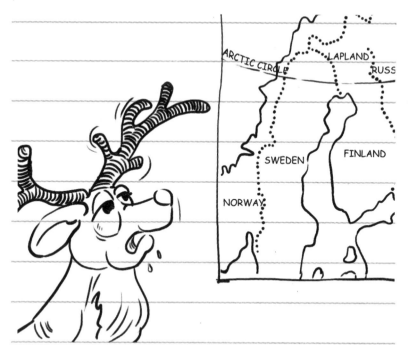

"Now, let me tell you about Lapland. I remember that the winters were very bad, you know, freezing winds, snow everywhere, and the days never started, so it was dark all the time.

"The summers were just the opposite; it was light all the time and I couldn't get any sleep. To be honest with you, I was getting bored with it.

"I had been told that Santa lived up there somewhere, but I had never seen him, or been invited to pull his sleigh.

"I had become fed up with my life. I wanted to get away from it. I needed to move south, to feel the sun on my back, to experience some fun

in my boring life. I tried to
explain this to my mother, but
she was not pleased.

"She just told me, 'You will get used to it, son.'

"But I didn't, so one day I packed my reindeer suitcase and set off with my mother's last piece of advice still ringing in my ears:

'Roger, do remember to read all the instruction labels!'

"You see, Robin, because I was not good at reading, I never even tried to read labels and instructions; in fact, I never bothered at all.

"I headed south for the sun and a new life. As I wandered further and further, there was less and less moss, and I became more and more hungry.

"I had already passed several roadside fast-food outlets without realising what they were. Eventually, my curiosity and hunger got the better of me and I went inside the next one. As I approached the counter, a young lad wearing a paper hat said,

'Hi deer, dude, what do you want?'

"I had no idea what I wanted and couldn't read the menu, but so that I didn't look stupid, I said, 'What have you got?'

"The lad reeled off a list of things called burgers. 'Okay,' I said, 'I'll have the first one you said.'

"I was then presented with a little cardboard box, so I sat down and ate it. The cardboard was alright, but I really didn't enjoy the filling; it was some sort of bread and meat thing ... maybe I should have tried to read the label.

"I walked on for several days. The weather had become warmer, the birds were singing and the sky was blue. I was in a lovely valley with lots of farms and pretty villages. Soon I found a cottage with a big garden to stay in.

"I was very happy there; this was the life for a young reindeer! I went to the local supermarket and came back with a trolley full of food, but I was not very keen on any of it.

"Everything tasted of cardboard and plastic; some of it was even rock hard, like frozen snow, and I didn't like it at all ... Maybe I should have read the labels. I began to miss nice tasty moss.

"Then I remembered an old uncle telling me about people who grew their own food; I thought they were a herd called the gardeners. I decided to give it a try.

"I went to the garden centre and looked around. There were lots of seed packets, but I didn't enjoy the taste of the paper, and they all had instructions printed on the back which I couldn't read.

"Then, in the corner, I saw something green, which was half grown already. I bought it all, and the man at the counter told me, 'Put it in the ground, put some fertiliser on it and it will grow.'

"So I went home with a
wheelbarrow full of the green
plants and a huge tub of
fertiliser.

"That evening, I did what the man had said; I planted the green things in the ground and then poured on the whole tub of fertiliser. I had completely forgotten what my mother told me about trying to read the instructions.

"I slept well that night and also halfway through the next day. When I eventually woke up in the afternoon, it was still quite dark, just like Lapland in the winter.

"When I got up and opened the curtains, it was still dark, and I wondered what was going on. Outside the window, the garden had become a jungle, and all that I could see were thick red stalks and giant leaves, which were blocking out the sun.

"I tried to open the back door, but it was blocked by the huge plants. Eventually, I managed to get out through the front window, but what a sight! The whole street was covered by these enormous plants. The neighbours were not amused at all. I stomped back to the garden centre to complain.

" 'Ah yes,' said the man, 'you are the reindeer who bought all the giant rhubarb. How much fertiliser did you put on it?'

"So I told him.

" 'What, the whole tub?' the man replied. 'It only needs half a cup; didn't you read the instruction label?'

"I have to tell you, I went back to the cottage feeling like a proper idiot, but at least I had plenty of rhubarb to eat, and so did all of my neighbours.

"I cut down huge sticks of the stuff and started to chew it. It was awful, so bitter and sour; I just couldn't eat it.

"By this time I was sick of cardboard, plastic and bitter rhubarb. I longed for the flavour of lush green moss. I was also getting tired of not being able to read and write. It was becoming embarrassing, and I was determined to do something about it.

"Somebody told me that the local library was running a special course called Reading and Writing for Reindeers, so I went along and joined straight away.

"I didn't find the lessons easy, but I was determined to get through the course, so I went to class every day and did all of the homework.

"And would you believe
it, by the end of the course I
could read and write perfectly.
And do you know what my
favourite things to read were?
Yes, you guessed it, labels!

"Then one morning, the letter box clunked and a letter dropped onto the mat. I was very excited as I opened it, and do you know who it was from?"

"No, Roger, we have no idea."

"Well, I shall tell you. It was from Santa. Yes, everyone writes letters to Santa, but not many people get a letter back!

"The letter said that there were problems in Lapland at his toy factory and he needed another reindeer who could read and write. I just couldn't believe my luck.

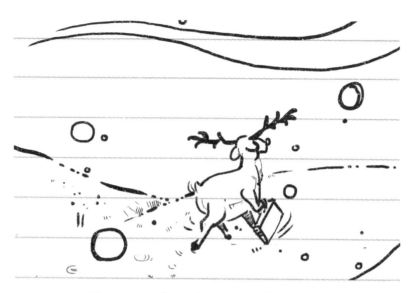

"I packed my little reindeer suitcase and headed back up north. Now, to cut a long story short, I worked with Santa for many years. I helped him with writing present labels and letters, and I also went with him on his Christmas deliveries.

"Eventually, I retired and he left me with some children in England, but after Christmas they got bored with me, so I ended up at the car boot sale with Mr Ben's Odds and Ends. And now I am here with you and Grandad. I hope you will be nice to me."

"Yes, of course, Roger, we are always nice to toys."

After Roger had finished his
story, Grandad took Robin home,
but he promised to come back
at the same time next Sunday.

It was the last week at school before the Christmas break. Final rehearsals were going on for the school nativity play, and some of the classes were going to see a pantomime.

Robin went to the playing field at break-time; he just wanted to sit down and check his letter to Santa. He was about to sit on the bench when he saw a sign: Wet Paint. *That was close*, he thought to himself.

Then Alicia arrived, and before he could stop her, she sat down on the freshly painted bench.

"No, Alicia, wait!" But it was too late.

She got up, but nothing could be done; her coat was ruined.

"Oh, my coat!" she said without thinking.

Robin was astonished to hear Alicia speak in English.

"I didn't think you could speak English," Robin said.

"I can speak a little."

"But you haven't learned to read yet."

"Reading in English is difficult, but I can read well in Italian."

"I can't read or write in Italian," said Robin, "and unfortunately, neither can the person who painted the bench. Would you like to come to my house after school and I can help you with your reading?"

Robin was the first friend that Alicia had made since she arrived in England, so she agreed. When she came round later that afternoon, they had some of Grandma's delicious mince pies, and then Roger the Reindeer told Alicia his story...

And then, with some help from Robin, Alicia wrote Christmas cards to her classmates ... in English!

Before Alicia left, she promised to ask her dad for special classes, and Robin was sure that she would be reading and writing in English in no time at all.

After Alicia had gone, Robin realised that he still hadn't thought of a Christmas present for Grandad, so he decided to ask Roger.

"Look, Roger, you are the expert on Christmas presents. What do you think my grandad would like this Christmas?"

"Well, Robin, I know what grandads like best. I know that he would love something which was made by you."

"Oh, right. What do you suggest then?"

"I know that you are very good at drawing, so why don't you do a drawing for Grandad and write your name on it?"

"That's a great idea!"

So that's what he did.
He drew a lovely picture of
Roger the Reindeer pulling
Santa's sleigh, wrote his name
on it and put it in a frame. And
do you know, that was the best
Christmas present Grandad
had ever been given.